Anansi and Sky King

Hare and Lion

Two Trickster Tales from Africa

retold by Cynthia Swain and Brooke Harris
illustrated by Sholto Walker

Table of Contents

Focus on the Genre: Trickster Tales 2
Meet Some Famous African Tricksters 4
Anansi and Sky King 6
Hare and Lion 14
The Writer's Craft: Trickster Tales 22
Glossary 24
Make Connections Across Texts. . . Inside Back Cover

TRICKSTER TALES

What is a trickster tale?

A trickster tale is a short story in which animals or other creatures talk, think, and act like people. One character, the trickster, uses clever pranks or traps to fool another character. Often the trickster is much smaller than the character he fools. Sometimes the trickster wants to help others, but other times the trickster only wants to help himself.

What is the purpose of a trickster tale?

A trickster tale shows human characteristics and problems in an entertaining way. A trickster tale often teaches a lesson. The tale shows what happens when people make bad choices—although some of the bad choices come from the tricksters themselves!

How do you read a trickster tale?

Pay attention to the title. The title will often tell you which character is the trickster. Each character stands for ways that humans behave. As you read, ask yourself, “What human quality, or trait, does each character represent?” Notice what happens to the main characters. Think about how the events in the story support the lesson that the tale tries to teach.

Features of a Trickster Tale

The story is short and usually funny.

The main characters are usually animals.

The trickster may have a flaw.

The trickster has a problem or helps someone with a problem.

The trickster outwits another character to solve the problem.

Who invented trickster tales?

Trickster tales originated all over the world, but African and Native American tales are among the most common today. The tales were originally passed down through oral storytelling. In modern times, many have been made into books and films. Some of today's popular cartoon characters are tricksters!

Meet Some Famous African Tricksters

Name: Anansi the Spider

His Life: Anansi (ah-NAHN-see) was a trickster hero of the Ashanti people in Ghana as well as the Akan people of West Africa. He was said to be the son of a sky god. People admired him because of his cleverness. However, they didn't truly approve of his trickery, which was often the result of greed.

Other African Spider Tricksters: The Zande people of Central Africa told stories of Ture the Spider. The Hausa people of West Africa had a trickster spider named Gizo.

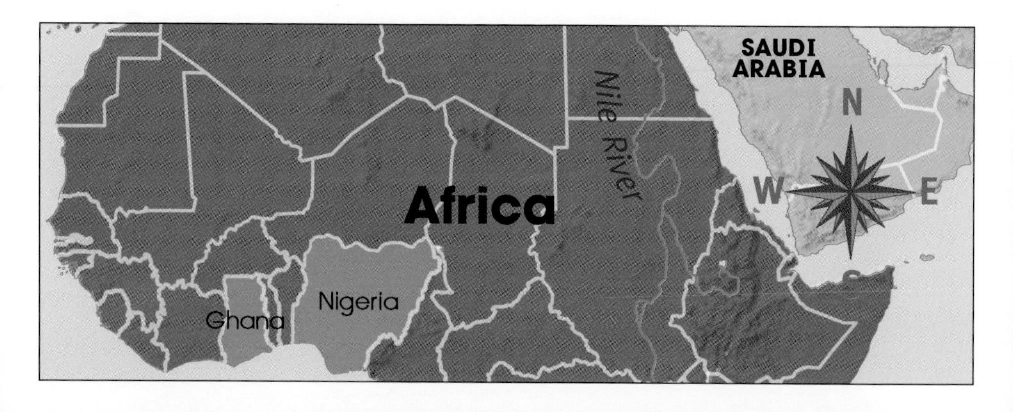

Name: Zomo

His Life: The hare Zomo (ZOH-moh) was a trickster hero of the Yoruba tribe of Nigeria. He wasn't big or strong, but he was clever. Many storytellers believe the original Zomo stories were meant to teach children that even though they were small, they could overcome great obstacles.

Other African Hare Tricksters: The Swahili people on the coast of East Africa told stories of Sungura the Hare. The Wolof people of Senegal had a trickster hare named Leuck. The trickster hare of the Bemba people of Zambia was Kalulu, and the trickster hare of the Baganda tribe of East Africa was Wakaima.

Tools Writers Use

Personification

Look at the word **personification** (per-sah-nuh-fih-KAY-shun). You will see the word **person** in it. **Personification** means giving human characteristics to animals or objects. In the trickster tales you read, notice how the animals talk, think, and act the way people do. Notice how animals are described as if they had human abilities. These are all examples of personification.

Anansi the spider was smart. He was the smartest animal in Africa. He loved to read. He loved stories best. But the king of the sky owned all stories. Even worse, Sky King was greedy. He would not share his stories. But that did not stop Anansi.

"Sky King," said Anansi, "I will buy your stories. What do you want for them?"

Sky King did not want to sell his stories. He did not want to be bugged by a spider. He wanted Anansi to go away. So Sky King told Anansi the stories would cost a lot. "Bring me Hornet. Bring me Snake. Bring me Leopard. They are strong. I want them for myself," said Sky King.

Getting those mean animals would be hard. But Anansi was not afraid. "I will outsmart them," he thought.

The next morning, Anansi went to Hornet's home. He knew that Hornet might sting him. He also knew that Hornet hated to get wet. Smart Anansi filled a bowl with water. Then he sprayed Hornet's nest.

"It's raining!" cried Anansi. "Come out, Hornet. You will drown!"

Hornet was wet. Hornet was mad. He was also a little scared. "Where can I go?"

"Fly into this dry bowl. I will save you," Anansi said.

"Good idea," said Hornet. He did as he was told.

Anansi quickly covered the bowl. "Got you!" The spider laughed. Then he brought Hornet to Sky King.

"Very good, Anansi," said Sky King. "I am pleased. One down, two to go."

Getting Hornet was pretty easy. Snake and Leopard would be hard to trick. But Anansi was **determined**. He would do whatever he needed. He would get the stories from Sky King.

But how? How could Anansi get Snake? Snake was strong. Snake was smart. Anansi used his brain. "Aha! Snake is proud. That is how I will trick him," Anansi thought.

Anansi picked up a stick. He went near Snake. He said loudly, "No! No! You are wrong!" He wanted Snake to hear him.

"What's wrong, Anansi?" asked Snake. "Why are you talking to yourself?"

"Oh, Snake, it is nothing. My wife and I had a fight. She says that you're not that big. She thinks that you are small. She says you are shorter than this stick. I said she is wrong."

Snake hissed. "She issss wrong. I am longer than that sssstick."

"Then we must prove it," Anansi said. "Lie down against the stick. We will see if you are longer." Snake did so.

"There's a problem," said Anansi. "You keep moving. Let me stretch you out. Let me tie you to the stick. Then we will know. Will you be right? Or will my wife be right?"

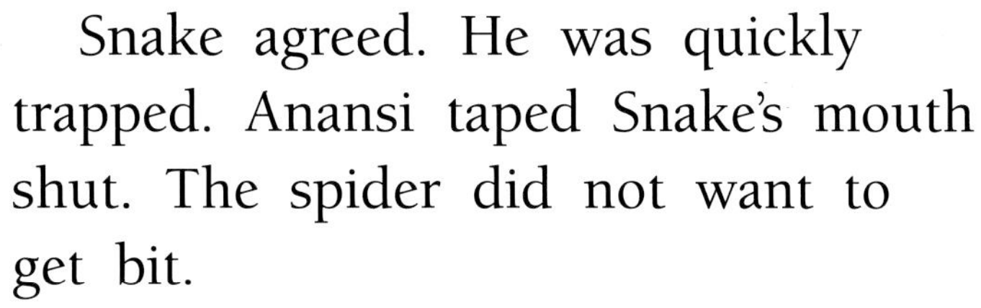

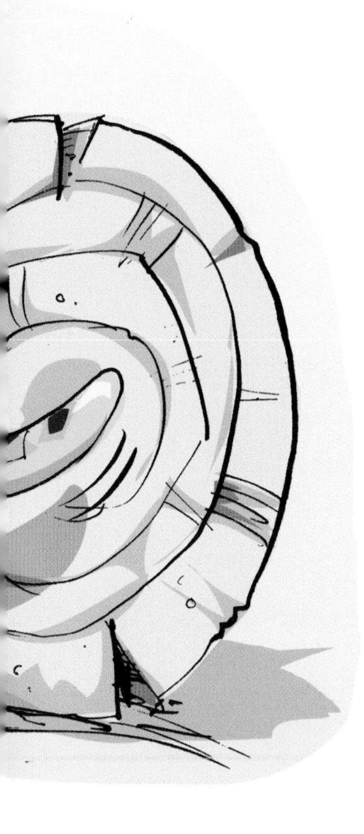

Snake agreed. He was quickly trapped. Anansi taped Snake's mouth shut. The spider did not want to get bit.

Anansi handed Snake to Sky King. He laughed and said, "Two down and one to go. Then all the stories will be mine, Sky King!"

"Don't be so **cocky**," said Sky King. "Leopard is **ferocious**. He is always angry. He will try to kill you. He will tear you apart."

Anansi stopped laughing. Leopard would be hard to capture. So Anansi hid in the grass. He watched Leopard take his daily walk.

Anansi's brain hummed as he watched. Soon, an idea leaped into his head. He would make a trap!

The next day, Anansi dug a hole. The hole was where Leopard liked to walk. Anansi covered the hole. He covered it with branches. Then he waited.

Finally, Leopard walked by. The big cat fell right into the hole!

"Hey! What the . . . ? OW!" cried Leopard.

Anansi called down to Leopard, "I see that you've fallen. Can I help you get out?"

Leopard trusted no one. But he could not get out. Leopard was **desperate**. He had no other choice. He didn't know what else to do. "Yes," he said. "I do need your help, spider!"

"There is only one way to lift you," said Anansi. "You must tie this rope around your tail. Then I will pull you up."

Leopard was not happy. Still, he tied the rope around his tail. Anansi pulled Leopard up halfway. Then Anansi twisted the rope. He turned the rope in circles. Leopard spun around. He got very dizzy. Leopard couldn't stand when he reached the top. Anansi dragged Leopard by the tail to Sky King.

"Great warriors tried to bring me Hornet, Snake, and Leopard," said Sky King. "They failed. You have succeeded. You are clever, Anansi. You are crafty. I do not want to give away my stories. But you earned them. Promise that you will share my stories. Give my stories to all who want them."

Analyze the Characters and Plot

- Who were the characters in the tale?
- Which character was the trickster? How do you know?
- Which animals did the trickster fool? What did he do?
- Why did the trickster fool these animals?

Analyze the Tools Writers Use

Personification

- During the story, when do the characters think like people?
- During the story, when do the characters express human emotions?
- How does personification make this story more interesting?

Focus on Words

Description

To describe is to tell what something is like. Authors use description to help readers picture people, animals, places, and objects in their minds. For example, in this tale, the author explains that the leopard was so dizzy he couldn't stand. Reread the trickster tale to find descriptions for the following story words.

Page	Word	Description
8	determined	
9	cocky	
9	ferocious	
11	desperate	

Hare and Lion

The setting and problem are stated in the first paragraph. The reader learns where the story takes place and what it will be about.

The authors use personification when they write, "Even the trees shook with fright." This gives the story a playful feel. Trickster tales are often funny.

A tiny village in Africa had a big problem. The animals wanted to live in peace. But each night, Lion came into the village. He caused awful **destruction**. He knocked down homes. He caught animals. He ate animals. Everyone lived in fear. Even the trees shook with fright when they heard Lion roar.

Cheetah called a meeting. All the animals came.

"We must find a way to stop Lion," said Cheetah. "No animal will be left alive. Our village will be empty."

“Let’s run away,” said Elephant. He always shared his ideas. Most of the time, his ideas were not so good.

“You are too noisy when you run,” said Cheetah. “Lion will hear you. He will follow us wherever we go.”

“What can we do?” cried the monkeys.

Zebra stood up. “I have an idea. Every night, one animal will go to Lion. That animal will be his dinner. Then Lion will leave us alone.”

“Will you go first? Do you want to be Lion’s dinner tonight?” Cheetah asked Zebra.

Zebra was silent. He did not want to be the first one eaten by Lion. He did not want to be eaten second, either. He did not want to be eaten third. He did not want to be eaten at all.

Hare was in the back. Hare was small. No one saw him until he spoke up.

The authors bring in the main character here. Hare wants to help his fellow animals, no matter how scary Lion is. Willingness to help others is a characteristic of trickster heroes.

"I will go," said Hare.

"Hare? Is that you?" asked Cheetah. "Come to the front. You will **sacrifice** yourself? For the village? Let us honor Hare. He is giving up his life for us."

The animals clapped. They cheered. They thanked Hare for his bravery. Some animals believed he was being foolish. But Hare was not a fool. Hare was clever.

The next day, Hare went to Lion's den.

Hares and other animals can't talk. This is another example of personification.

"Lion, let's make a deal. Every day, one animal will visit you. He will be your meal. For that, you must leave our village alone. I am here to be your first meal."

"You must be joking," said Lion. "You are so small. I would need to eat a hundred of you before I am full. Did you bring ninety-nine others like you?"

"Well, if you must know," said Hare, "I did. There were one hundred of us. But another lion met us on the way. He said he was the bravest lion around. He **devoured** all my friends. He didn't eat me because I hid."

Hare is not only brave, but he is also very clever. This is another feature of a trickster hero.

Lion roared. He was mad. "Another lion says he is braver than me? Ha! This other lion is pretending to be something he is not. Show me this **impostor**. I will prove how mighty I am. ROAR!"

The authors show that Lion has a flaw: He thinks he is the best lion around. Hare will use his knowledge of Lion's flaw to pull off his trick.

The authors bring in a new setting and a new event. Something new is going to happen to the characters.

"That lion lives in the river. The one near the waterfall," said Hare.

"Let's go," said Lion.

Hare led Lion to the river. "There he is," said Hare. He pointed into the water. Lion stood at the bank. Lion looked into the water. He saw a mean lion looking back!

The authors give Hare a line of dialogue that convinces Lion to jump into the water. Instead of telling the reader what Hare does, they let Hare do the talking, which shows how clever he is.

"Stop hiding in the water! You are a coward," called Lion. "Come out and fight!"

The lion in the water hardly moved. "He must be afraid of you," said Hare. "Surely he is no match for you."

“Then I will get him,” said Lion. He jumped into the river.

Splash! Lion hit the water. He soon sank.

“Hey! I can’t swim!” he cried. “And where did that other lion go?”

There was no other lion living in the river. Lion had seen his own reflection in the water. Hare had tricked Lion!

Lion floats far away. The problem of the story is solved: Hare is the trickster hero who saves the village.

Lion came up for air. Then the river carried him away. Lion went over the waterfall. Lion was gone.

Hare ran back to the village. He told everyone the good news. All the animals **celebrated**. They had a big party. They danced. They sang. They ate. Then they danced some more.

Reread the Trickster Tale

Analyze the Characters and Plot

- Who were the characters in the tale?
- Which character was the trickster? How do you know?
- Who did the trickster fool? What did he do?
- How did the trickster help the other animals?

Analyze the Tools Writers Use

Personification

Find these examples of personification, then explain why they are personification.

- Lion and Hare speak to each other.
- Hare thinks like a human.
- The characters show feelings.

Focus on Words

Description

Look for descriptions in the trickster tale to help you understand each story word below.

Page	Word	Description
14	destruction	
16	sacrifice	
17	devoured	
17	impostor	
20	celebrated	

How does an author write a TRICKSTER TALE?

Reread "Hare and Lion" and think about what the authors did to write this tale. How did they develop the story? How can you, as a writer, develop your own trickster tale?

Decide on a Problem

Remember: A trickster tale solves a problem. In "Hare and Lion," the authors wanted to show that someone small and weak could help his friends by outsmarting someone big and strong.

Brainstorm Characters

Writers ask these questions:

- What kind of animal or creature is my trickster?
- What human traits does my trickster have?
- How does my trickster show that he or she is clever? What does he or she do, say, or think?
- What other characters will be important to my story? Which character will the trickster try to fool? Which characters will benefit from the trickster's acts?

Character	Traits	Actions Based on Traits
Hare	clever; brave	tricked lion to save the animals
Lion	cruel; proud; jealous	wanted to eat all one hundred rabbits

Brainstorm Setting and Plot

Writers ask these questions:

- Where does my trickster tale take place? How will I describe it?
- What is the problem, or situation?
- How does the main character's cleverness affect the events in the story?
- What events happen?
- How does the tale end?

Complete a graphic organizer like the one below.

Setting	a tiny village where many animals live together
Problem of the Story	Lion visits the village every night to get animals to eat.
Story Events	1. The animals have a meeting to try to decide what to do about Lion. 2. Hare says he will offer himself as food for Lion—but he really has another plan in mind. 3. Hare visits Lion and tells him another lion has eaten the ninety-nine rabbits that came with him.
Solution to the Problem	Hare leads Lion to the river. Lion thinks his reflection is his competitor. He jumps in and the river takes him far away.

Glossary

celebrated (SEH-luh-bray-ted) praised or honored (page 20)

cocky (KAH-kee) boldly confident (page 9)

desperate (DES-puh-rit) having no hope (page 11)

destruction (dih-STRUK-shun) the act of destroying something (page 14)

determined (dih-TER-mend) driven to succeed (page 8)

devoured (dih-VOW-erd) ate up greedily (page 17)

ferocious (fuh-ROH-shus) very mean (page 9)

impostor (im-PAHS-ter) someone who pretends to be something else (page 17)

sacrifice (SA-kruh-fise) an offering (page 16)